FARM ANIMALS

Text by F. Pezzoli and E. Mora

Illustrations by Kennedy

Translation by Jean Grasso Fitzpatrick

BARRON'S

New York/London/Toronto/Sydney

THE ROOSTER

The sprightly, colorful rooster stands as proud and straight as a soldier. Every morning he cries "Cock-a-doodle-doo!" from the center of the barnyard. When the sun comes up it's his job to call the farmer back to work.

All the other birds in the barnyard wake up, too—the chickens, geese, ducks, and turkeys. They run around and scratch the dirt searching for grain and small worms. Sometimes they start fighting over an especially tasty-looking morsel of food. Then the rooster, king of the chicken coop, settles the matter. But he doesn't take sides. He ends the battle by giving everyone a good pecking.

Of course, the rooster gets hungry, too. He eats grain, earthworms, and even pebbles. He can crush almost anything in his beak, which is as hard as stone.

Just look at him! He has strong feet with sharp points called spurs. The rooster uses these as weapons. The rooster also has a magnificent tail with feathers of many different colors. On his head he has a fiery-red crest and a red "beard" called a wattle.

The rooster struts around looking majestic. He seems to think he is better than all the other animals. Maybe he thinks that without him to watch over them and tell them all what to do, life in the barnyard would come to an end.

THE GOAT

The goat has done its day's work. It has given its rich, creamy milk to its master, and now it looks as though it's ready to take a walk. Where is it going? Probably into the forest. This animal is very fond of the tender little branches and bark of young trees. It also likes to nibble the tops of small shrubs. But its mischief doesn't end there—it also tramples tiny seedlings with its hooves. The farmer doesn't like any of these tricks very much.

The goat is a very nimble creature. It can go up and down steep hills with no trouble at all.

Some people think that the goat is an odd animal. But look at that mop of hair, those twisted horns, and that funny beard! Doesn't it remind you of a kindly old grandfather?

THE RABBIT

Do you see how happy the rabbit is with its supply of food? This animal is known for its hearty appetite. Its jaws are constantly moving. This is because its sharp teeth are always growing, and it has to gnaw to keep them short. That's one reason why the rabbit eats all the time.

THE HORSE

This animal has a rather long head. Its eyes are big and wide, and it often flares its damp, black nostrils. The horse walks on one toe at a time. This toe is very strong and is covered with a thick, hard toenail called a hoof.

Look at the horse's ears. They are short, thin, and very sensitive. A good jockey knows his or her own horse by the way it moves its ears!

Look again—do you see the magnificent mane along the back of the horse's neck, and its thick tail? They make this animal look rather noble.

The horse always looks beautiful, whether it is trotting, galloping, neighing—or even kicking!

The baby horse, which is called a colt, is also nice and frisky. Have you ever seen one skipping next to its mother? Didn't it look awkward, as though its legs were too long for its body?

THE DONKEY

The donkey is like a poor cousin to the horse. It is short and stocky and does not look at all noble like the horse. Its tail is much plainer, and its coat is a boring gray. It has very long ears that move around a lot.

The donkey's master can guess its mood by looking at those ears. If the donkey keeps them straight, it is calm. In moments of fear, it brings them forward as if to defend itself. If it is nervous, it draws them back to show rebellion or anger.

Like the horse, the donkey is very useful to people. But people are not always very nice to this hard-working animal. Does it seem fair to call a student who doesn't want to study a "donkey"?

THE DOG

Here's Fido at his workplace. Although he doesn't look very ferocious, he's a guard dog.

That's only one of the jobs a dog can do. Dogs can also hunt, or watch over a flock of sheep. A St. Bernard dog is an expert at finding travelers buried in the snow. At the movies you may have seen how helpful a police dog can be! And let's not forget the seeing-eye dogs who guide blind people.

The dog has a very expressive voice that it uses in many different ways. It growls angrily at strangers, and barks joyfully as it runs to meet its master. When it defends a bone, it snarls. And when it howls, it seems to be begging for pity.

The dog really is our best friend. It does whatever we ask it to do. It helps us, defends us, and loves us. A dog is faithful to its master its whole life long.

But above all the dog is a child's best friend. Do you have a dog? Doesn't it always want to play games with you? When it runs to meet you, see how it wags its tail. Don't worry if it nips at you happily. It's just being friendly!

THE DUCKLINGS

Here are the ducklings, the baby ducks, having a good time in the water.

They have wide, flat beaks, short necks, and chubby little bodies. Their legs are short. And they have webbed feet, which means there are strips of skin between their toes. This helps make them very good swimmers.

You often see ducklings floating in the water behind their mother, looking for food. They eat small fish, tadpoles, worms, insects, and water grasses. When they see something they want to eat, they dive into the water and catch the food with their beaks.

THE HEN

This bird looks rather plain and homely. The only touch of color on her body is the red of her crest and her "beard" or wattle. What a contrast with the proud rooster and his colorful feathers!

Let's watch the hen at home on the farm.

The farmer's wife has just opened the door to the henhouse. Out pops the hen into the barnyard. She takes a drink at the trough, which is full of rainwater.

Now the hen can go for a nice, long walk. She has been sitting on her eggs for twenty days without a break. She never left the nest in all that time. But now the eggs have hatched, and here are the little chicks! They are all yellow and peeping as they take their first steps in the barnyard. The mother takes care of them, and pecks at the ground with her beak to teach them how to find grain, little worms, and tender fresh grass to eat.

When the hen walks, she lifts her stiff feet and puts them down slowly. With each step she reaches out her toes and scratches for food.

As evening falls, the mother hen gathers her chicks under her wings. They feel right at home there, just like all children. When it's dark, don't you like to be home with your mother?

THE MOUSE

The mouse is a small rodent with a pointed snout and a long, thin tail.

The newborn mouse is as weak and helpless as a tiny kitten, which is its natural enemy, of course! It needs its mother until it has grown up enough to take care of itself. But when it grows up, it can do all sorts of things. It can run, jump, climb, and swim very well. And it can slip into the tiniest holes.

The mouse is smart and brave, but it also knows when to be cautious. It lives in houses, stables, meadows, fields, and forests. It is not at all afraid of the dark—in fact, it often makes its home in dark places.

The mouse lives to be three years old. And it spends most of its life bothering people. It even nibbles at things it can't eat, like wood and paper.

The mouse is not very useful to people. That's why we use cats to catch mice, and set traps for them. We put pieces of cheese into the traps. That attracts the mice, because they are very fond of cheese.

THE PIG

You can't have a farm without a pig. You can always hear it grunting, and see it rubbing its nose into the ground as it looks for food.

The pig has small eyes, and ears that look straight and pointy sometimes, broad and droopy at other times. Its nose looks almost like an elephant's trunk that has been flattened at the end. Its tail is short and curly.

The pig eats fattening foods. It is considered a greedy animal because it has such a big appetite.

Because it loves to roll in the mud, people think of the pig as a dirty animal. But it does that to keep cool and to get rid of the insects that bother it. Still, when a child gets all dirty, people say, "What a little piggy you are!"

THE CAT

The cat likes to walk around the house on its soft feet. Its glowing eyes can see even in the dark. They seem to see everything.

The cat is very, very agile and can jump surprisingly fast. It loves to play with a ball of yarn. It runs and kicks the ball with its sharp claws. But it can also pull these claws back inside its paws, which are protected by special pads. That is why the cat is able to walk so quietly.

When the cat feels tired, it looks around for a comfortable place, curls up and falls asleep. When it wakes up, it meows for attention. If you run your hand along its back and rub its silky fur, it purrs and feels happy.

The cat is sweet and affectionate to you. But it isn't at all kind to its enemy, the mouse. After a cat catches a mouse, it plays a game. First it pretends to let the mouse go free. Then it catches the mouse again with its paws. It does that over and over again. When it is tired, the cat stops playing and kills the mouse. Because mice can be a real nuisance, the farmer is glad that cats are such good mouse hunters.

THE COW

If you look at her, the cow's big eyes and kind face seem to say that she could never be mean to you.

And it's true. The cow gives us wonderful, healthful milk to drink. We also use milk to make butter and all the different kinds of cheeses.

Here she comes, slowly walking in the grass with her nose to the ground. She pulls up tufts of grass and swallows them almost whole, putting them in a part of her stomach called the rumen.

Later, she brings the grass back into her mouth a little bit at a time. She chews and chews peacefully. This is called ruminating, and many animals that eat grass do it.

When we see the cow in the barn, her big, plain body is stretched out on the hay. Her head, with its bent horns, is turned to the calf beside her. It was just born. It looks at her with sweet eyes, and moos softly.

The farmers love this quiet, gentle animal. They give her names that show how close they feel to her—Daisy, Bessie, or Belle.

THE SHEEP

The sheep is a very shy and fearful animal. When it is frightened, it starts to bleat: "Baa, baa!" It is always getting lost, and sometimes it gets into real danger.

Every spring, the sheep is shorn. That means that its soft wool is cut off. When winter comes the wool has already grown back, to keep the animal snug and warm.

The sheep eats grasses, roots, and small branches, and also loves salt. It lives with other sheep in a flock.

The young sheep are called lambs. They are very pretty, and their wool is especially soft and light. As soon as they are born, they try to stand up on their weak legs and take their first wobbly steps. Soon they become lively and can play and skip in the meadow.

In the summer the shepherds bring the flocks to graze on the mountains, but in the fall they lead them back down to the plains. Sometimes you see a sheep dog or a donkey with a flock of sheep. The sheep dog's job is to watch over the sheep and keep them together. The donkey takes care of the little lambs that are not strong enough to move around with the rest of the flock.

THE GOOSE

The goose is the guard of the barnyard. It struts around importantly, watching everything that's going on.

Every so often it likes to dive into a pond. It has two webbed feet, and the skin stretched between its toes helps it swim. The goose's feathers never get wet because they are covered with special oil. So the water rolls right off its back!

The mother goose leads her little goslings to the water. She tells them not to be afraid, and she teaches them to get food. She cheers on the timid goslings and holds back the wild ones. If they go too far away, she calls them back. "Here, here," she says. The little white puffballs come running to her calls.

The goose gives us lovely big eggs. And its feathers make your pillow warm and soft to give you a good night's sleep!